This book is dedicated to my Peace Class students, whose many acts of kindness inspired this story. Thank you for reminding me that goodness is all around us.

—LR

HENRY

IS

KIND

A Story of Mindfulness

WRITTEN BY **LINDA RYDEN**

ILLUSTRATED BY **SHEARRY MALONE**

TILBURY HOUSE PUBLISHERS, THOMASTON, MAINE

PLANT KINDNESS AND GATHER LOVE.

YOU COULD •PLAY• WITH SOMEONE WHO LOOKS LONELY.

"Good morning, class!" said Ms. Snowden.

"Can you all take your seats on the rug for mindfulness practice? Remember, this is the time we set aside each day to slow down and pay attention to our bodies, hearts, and minds. Today we are going to do a new kind of mindfulness practice called Heartfulness, which helps us be kinder to ourselves and each other."

"So let's go into our Mindful Bodies. Close your eyes and take three deep breaths.

"Now think of someone who makes you happy—someone in your family, someone in this class, or even a pet.

"Have you thought of someone?"

"I'll say words out loud, and you can think them while picturing your family member or friend or pet in your mind. If you want to, you can put your hand over your heart."

NO ACT OF KINDNESS, NO MATTER HOW SMALL, IS EVER WASTED.

HEARTFULNESS :

· MAY YOU BE HAPPY
· MAY YOU BE HEALTHY AND STRONG
· MAY YOU BE PEACEFUL

Ms. Snowden said, "May you be happy."

In their minds, everyone thought those words for someone who made them happy.

Ms. Snowden said, "May you be healthy and strong." Everyone thought those words.

Ms. Snowden said, "May you be peaceful."

Then Ms. Snowden said, "Try to notice how it made you feel to think those kind thoughts. Any way that you feel is just fine. Just try to notice it."

When Ms. Snowden rang the little bell to end their Mindfulness practice, everyone opened their eyes.

"Does anyone want to share who they were thinking about?" Ms. Snowden asked.

Doris said, "I was thinking about my brother DeWayne. Sometimes he gets on my nerves, but most of the time he makes me happy."

Alice said, "I was thinking about my mom. She made me pancakes for breakfast this morning—on a school day!"

Dhruv said, "I was thinking about my little sister Sonali. It felt weird at first, but then it made me feel happy. She's pretty cool for a little sister."

Henry said, "I was thinking about my Rubik's Cube!"

Everyone laughed, but Ms. Snowden said, "That's fine, Henry. I know that your Rubik's Cube is important to you."

THE KINDNESS PROJECT

Ms. Snowden said, "Thinking kind thoughts about people we love can make us feel really good and want to do kind things. We can even send kind thoughts to ourselves. Speaking of kindness, can anybody think of something kind they did this week?"

Edwin raised his hand. "I feed my cat every day. Is that a kind thing?"

"Yes!" said Ms. Snowden. "Taking care of your cat is an act of kindness." Edwin smiled.

"You are all doing an act of kindness right now by listening to me mindfully. Really paying attention to another person is an act of kindness," said Ms. Snowden. The children looked at each other proudly.

"So today we are going to start a Kindness Project," she said. "This week I want you to think of a kind act to do, and then, after you do it, draw a picture of it. Next week we'll share our pictures and hang them on the bulletin board in the hallway."

Everybody was excited about the Kindness Project.

Alice raced home after school. She knew exactly what she wanted to do. When it was time for dinner, she told her dad that she was going to set the table. She put out a fancy blue tablecloth and green napkins that she folded carefully.

On Saturday, Doris gave her brother DeWayne a balloon with a peace sign on it.

Rosie carried her neighbor Glenn's newspaper right up to his door.

Yoab and his friend Jonah cleaned up trash in the park near their school.

Andrew stayed after school and sharpened all of Ms. Snowden's pencils.

Next week in class, everyone shared
their Kindness Project pictures.

Henry thought about all the other kids sharing their acts of kindness. He felt awful.

Ms. Snowden said, "Henry, I'm sure you can think of something kind you did . . . ."

"No I can't!" yelled Henry. "Kindness is stupid!" He headed toward the classroom door.

The class was silent for a moment. Then Rosie raised her hand and Ms. Snowden said, "Yes, Rosie?"

"Henry," said Rosie, "don't you remember when we were in the library and you reached a book on the high shelf for me? That was kind."

Henry stopped just before
he reached the door.

Doris raised her hand too. "And remember when I didn't have a snack and you gave me your cookie?

"That was kind."

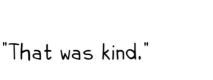

Henry turned and began
to smile just a little.

"Remember when you showed me how to make an origami swan?" said Edwin.

"Remember when you invited me to play basketball when I was new?" said Alice.

Henry looked a bit surprised. He said, "I let my sister play with my Rubik's Cube. Was that kind?"

"Yes, Henry. Sharing is kind!" said Ms. Snowden. "It sounds like you have done many acts of kindness. How did you feel when you did those things?"

"Good, I guess," said Henry. "It's funny that doing things for other people makes me feel good."

"That's the great thing about kindness," said Ms. Snowden.

THE KINDNESS PROJECT

"When you are kind to others, you make them happy and you make yourself happy too."

Alice said, "Just like when we did Heartfulness!"

"That's right, Alice," said Ms. Snowden.

Doris said, "I want to do more kind things. Can we keep doing this project?"

"Of course we can," said Ms. Snowden.
"Let's go out and fill the world with kindness!"

Later, at recess, Henry was flying paper airplanes with Dhruv. Dhruv's airplane flew fast and straight, but Henry's airplane kept flying back to him. Henry laughed and said, "I think I'll call this airplane Kindness, because when I send it out it always comes back to me!"

"That's cool," said Dhruv. "Can you teach me how to make my plane do that too?"

"Sure," said Henry. "I'd be happy to help!"

THE END

MINDFULNESS and HEARTFULNESS

I have been teaching mindfulness, including heartfulness, to my students at Lafayette Elementary School in Washington DC since 2003. Heartfulness, a sort of compassion meditation, is a simple but powerful practice that increases feelings of empathy, happiness, and connection with others, and the children in my classes love to do it. I include heartfulness as a foundational practice in my elementary school curriculum *Peace of Mind,* and I wrote *Henry Is Kind* to share this practice beyond the classroom. At home or in a school, it might go like this:

Sit up straight but comfortably and close your eyes. Think of someone you care about—a friend or a family member. What does it feel like to think about that person? Repeat these words in your mind:

May you be happy. May you be healthy and strong. May you be peaceful.

How does that make you feel? Any way you feel is fine. Think about yourself and give yourself a little hug if you want to. Repeat these words:

May I be happy. May I be healthy and strong. May I be peaceful.

How does this make you feel? Some people are uncomfortable with sending themselves kind thoughts. This is normal, but try it anyway. It might get easier with practice. Now think about all beings—all the people, animals, plants, everything alive in the world. Repeat these words:

May all beings be happy *(or all people or everyone on earth or whatever you'd like to say).* **May all beings be healthy and strong. May all beings be peaceful.**

How does it feel to think these thoughts? Open your eyes. You've practiced Heartfulness!

You can practice just one step at a time instead of all three. Or you might add more steps. You might send kind thoughts to a cashier at the grocery store, a letter carrier, or another person you've encountered recently. You might send good thoughts to a difficult person, even someone you're in

conflict with. Sending kind thoughts to someone you are in conflict with can be very powerful and go a long way toward helping
you deal with angry feelings. It may soften your feelings toward that
person, or remind you what you like about him or her, or give you a
chance to remember that we're all human and we all make mistakes.

Over the years I have seen my students' practice of mindfulness,
and in particular heartfulness, contribute to a more caring class-
room and a more positive school climate. It comes as no surprise to me that scholarly research has
confirmed these results. In their groundbreaking book *Altered Traits*, Richard Davidson and Daniel
Goleman identify research studies that meet the highest scientific standards and confirm that "compassion meditation enhances empathic concern, activates [brain] circuits for good feelings and love,
as well as circuits that register the suffering of others, and prepares a person to act when suffering is
encountered." These are profound results from a simple practice.

If you are interested in learning more about compassion meditation, you might enjoy the work of
author and teacher Sharon Salzberg, whom you can visit at www.SharonSalzberg.com.

For more information on mindfulness and compassion practice for children and in schools, you
might like to explore these resources, starting with my Peace of Mind website:

The Peace of Mind Program
https://teachpeaceofmind.org

Center for Healthy Minds, University of Wisconsin-Madison
https://centerforhealthy minds.org

Center for Compassion and Altruism Research and Education, Stanford University
http://ccare.stanford.edu

The Greater Good Science Center at the UC Berkeley
https://greatergood.berkeley.edu/topic/compassion

May we all be happy, healthy, strong, and peaceful!

Tilbury House Publishers
12 Starr Street
Thomaston, Maine 04861
800-582-1899 • www.tilburyhouse.com

Text © 2018 by Linda Ryden
Illustrations © 2018 by Shearry Malone

Hardcover ISBN 978-0-88448-661-9
eBook ISBN 978-0-88448-663-3

First hardcover printing August 2018

15 16 17 18 19 20 XXX 10 9 8 7 6 5 4 3 2 1

Library of Congress Control Number: 2018944767

Designed by Frame25 Productions
Printed in Korea

LINDA RYDEN is the full-time Peace Teacher at Lafayette Elementary School, a public school in Washington, DC, where she teaches weekly 45-minute classes to more than 600 children. She is also the creator of the Peace of Mind program and curriculum series, which includes *Peace of Mind: Core Curriculum for Grades 1 and 2* and *Peace of Mind: Core Curriculum for Grades 3-5*. Her work has been recognized in the *Washington Post* and the *Huffington Post*, and her program has been featured on local CBS, ABC and Fox5 news stations. Linda's books include *Rosie's Brain*, which uses a humorous story to introduce elementary school students to mindfulness skills. She is also the author of the forthcoming Tilbury House books *Sergio Sees the Good* and *Tyaja Uses the Think Test*. Visit www.TeachPeaceofMind.com for more.

SHEARRY MALONE studied art at Lipscomb University in Nashville. She is the illustrator of the *Absolutely Alfie* books, a spinoff from the *EllRay* Jakes series. Shearry's style is reminiscent of Quentin Blake's loose, quirky, timeless illustrations for books by Roald Dahl and others.